Thomas A. Kempis

Ayshu

Pausefully

Published by Pausefully, New York, NY.

ISBN: 978-1-892482-31-0

In the remote province of Judea,
the Roman rulers spoke Latin,
the cultivated elite Greek,
the priests Hebrew,
and the common folk Aramaic.

The two tales in this book are about
the extraordinary adventures of an
imaginary character, Ayshu. His Aramaic
name is rendered in Hebrew as Y'shua,
in Greek as Iesous and in Latin as Iesus.

Ayshu's life

This tale is loosely based on stories that have been floating in the Collective Implicit for a long time.

Mary Mog

There once was a time when very old men would marry sweet young things. And so it was that Mary Mog became old Joe Carpenter's wife.

Their union was blessed—or was it? On the one hand, they had a son. But, on the other hand, nothing seemed to go right from the moment they were married. And it kept getting worse after Ayshu's birth.

Here they were, wandering through the country, at a time when what you'd most want to do is feather your nest. Because of little Ayshu, they had to flee like criminals.

They'd arrive in a village in the evening, settle down in an abandoned shed or barn, and old Joe would go to the local inn. More often than not, he'd run back, very agitated. He'd be rushing Mary to get up and go. He had heard bad news, they had to leave right away, hush, hush, in the middle of the night, and go hide somewhere else.

Mary Mog knew it was for her child's sake that they were on the run, but still! What an irony! She had married the old man because it meant security, stability, and here she was, giving birth in a barn, far from friends and family, and no end in sight to this errant life.

The Announcement

Ayshu was older now, no longer a kid but not quite a man.

Mary Mog said to him: "*Son, you have reached the age of reason. It's time you and I have a talk*".

Parents say ominous things like that, not realizing how scary it feels to the kids.

"*Dad is not your real Dad*".

Jerry Behoovah

In the beginning, even before the beginning, way back when, there was Jerry Behoovah, who later became known as *Abba*—an Aramaic word that translates as *Good Old Dad*.

He felt very alone, and so he created a whole Universe: the Light and the Dark, the Earth and the Sea, and all the creatures that would inhabit the Earth.

But despite all this multitude, Jerry Behoovah still felt lonely. There was nobody in the whole wide world that could understand him.

Worship him, sure!
But understanding him was beyond them.

Jerry's yearning:

*"Oh just once
to be seen,
really seen
for who I am!*

*"If only I were
a carpenter..."*

Song of songs

"Marry me", said Jerry B. to Joe's wife.

"But what about Joe?", she asked.

"I have chosen you to have my child"

There was a gleam in her eyes: Happiness mixed with all the sadness in the world.

And so it came to be that
Mary had a little lamb.

The black sheep

The Lady Magdalene was reviled by the Righteous. But the Lamb befriended the Black Sheep.

And Ayshu heard her lament:

"They say I am a fallen woman. In this world,
I am a fallen person because I am a woman.

"A woman has no power. Except when she begets a powerful son."

Destiny

When Ayshu was a little baby, his Mama would cradle him in her arms and sing softly to him.

These were bittersweet songs about their life as lone wanderers, running away from powerful and ruthless enemies, running in accordance with Abba's will, selected by Abba to be His own very special runaways.

"You'll have to hide, my baby boy", she'd whisper. *"Until, one day, the world is safe.*

Then, the sun will shine, the birds will sing and the people will smile. They'll wave at you and shout Alleluia. There will be tears in your eyes. And there will be tears in my eyes as I see you basking in the love of the people and radiating love."

Little Ayshu grew up feeling really special. Whatever was happening to the family, to the whole wide world, seemed to revolve around him.

And so it came to be that, at the age of thirty-something, Ayshu was nailed to a Cross, wondering about that special destiny of his.

On the cross

First, he tried to resist the pain. Then, to ride it.

Then, he became the pain, the throbbing pain that started from his hands and legs and had taken over his belly, his chest, his head…

He screamed, he banged his head against the cross, trying to silence the explosions inside. To no avail.

Mary Mog and the Wailers, who had been kneeling at the foot of the cross for so long, no longer had any tears left.

Even the soldiers had tired of jeering; they were whiling away the time with a game of dice.

Ayshu once had fire in his eyes, a fire that would light a fire in others' eyes. But now his eyes looked dead.

Ayshu's lips moved.

A faint sound came out:

"Why...?"

Ayshu and Abba

Ayshu was now reunited with Abba. He kept asking questions, just like any child who is trying to make sense of the world.

Ayshu, a kid? Compared to *Good Old Dad*, who is not a kid?

He cried: *"Why did you forsake me?"*

Abba was so moved that, for once, he showed vulnerability: *"I failed you, my son."*

Good Tidings

One day, Ayshu appeared to his followers. At first, they did not recognize him, and asked: *"Who are you?"*

He said: *"I am"*.

And they knelt before him who is.

But, with a gesture of the hand, he bade them to stand up: *"So are you"*.

The second life of Ayshu

This tale is a recounting of a vision in
which I saw Aishu come back to life.

In the beginning, there was the Word.
The word came not from Above
but from the Gut. And the Word was:
"No!"

The Word is what brought Ayshu back
to life, what gave him a second life, when he was all
but dead.

I will now tell you how it came to be, as I saw it in
many a dream.

The vision starts with a face, close up. Darkish skin, bearded, longish hair. Thirty-something. Obviously in pain. A crown of thorns on his head. This is weird – why is the guy wearing, of all things, a crown of thorns?

Now, I see more of the scene. Weirder and weirder. The guy's actually carrying some wooden contraption that looks incredibly heavy – much, much bigger than he is. And this guy's not the body-builder type. No way he could pull that off.

On the other hand, his face looks convincing. Pain and dignity. Inner strength, that sort of thing. So, yes, it is believable after all.

There are crowds on each side of the cobblestone streets, jeering, taunting. Faces ranging from the ordinary to the vulgar. And soldiers, covered in shining armors.

Prodding the guy who's carrying this big burdensome piece of wood, stoically moving on toward his destiny.

This guy, of course, is Ayshu.

The big piece of wood is now on the ground. Ayshu is lying on it. And – uughh! One soldier is holding Ayshu's hand in place while another is placing a big carpenter's nail over his palm. Ayshu's arm tenses up, in pain, and blood splatters over the arm. Gross doesn't even begin to describe it.

Now Ayshu has started screaming – a bone-chilling howl that doesn't stop. It goes on as several soldiers are raising the cross, Ayshu is nailed onto it, writhing in pain.

Time passes. Ayshu is pulled down by his own weight, enlarging the wounds in his hands and feet, making his pain ever more excruciating. Flies are buzzing around him in the hot sun.

Ayshu is hanging on the cross. His face is twisted with pain, his eyes closed.

There's no spark in them, and no sound coming out of his throat, except an intermittent, pathetic moan.

Has he already given up the ghost? No, I now see his face hardened with an unmistakable expression of anger. A bloodcurdling shout comes out: "No!"

Anger travels through the dead muscles of his arms and legs. Muscles now bulging like they had never before, pulling his hand and legs through the nails that had bound them to the cross.

Ayshu is now standing at the foot of the cross. Standing in a gutter of blood, waving bloody hands, roaring: "No!"

The soldiers run away, and so do the rare onlookers.

Ayshu collapses into the soldiers' tent. And sleeps. He sleeps and sleeps, between life and death, for three days.

Ayshu stayed between life and death for three days, alternating between comatose sleep and bouts of high fever that drained whatever water was left in his body after he'd baked in the sun, nailed to the cross for a whole day.

When he opened his eyes, the first thing he saw was the caked wounds of his hands. He couldn't quite feel them yet—the pain would come back soon enough—but the mere sight of the wounds brought back to him the horrible reality of what he'd been through.

He started moving on his hands and knees, exploring the soldiers' tent. There was some wine and bread under a tarp. He first went to the bottle, tried to grab it with his open hand, only to howl in pain.

He would now have to teach himself new ways to do the simplest things. Sitting down, arms extended, holding the bottle with his extended fingertips, exerting as little pressure as possible to control the pain, he managed to open it.

Boy, did the wine feel good!

The sweetness, the warmth of it, how it lifted his spirits! And how good the bread—old and stale that it was!

He rolled over on the ground, grunted, and fell asleep.

Minutes or hours later, he woke up, feeling something wet going back and forth on his cheek. A donkey, entering its head through the opening of the tent, was licking him.

He suddenly realized how hopeless his situation would have been without this donkey: The wounds on his feet made it impossible for him to walk anywhere. He'd be dying of hunger and thirst...

Getting up on the donkey wasn't easy. Ayshu first tried standing on his toes, balancing himself with his extended fingertips against the donkey's body. But he couldn't manage to stay on tiptoe while raising one leg high enough to climb onto the donkey's back. Wine was helping him deal with the pain, but not with his balance.

Donkeys are not prone to learning new tricks. So, despite its good nature, this donkey wasn't doing much to help Ayshu. But, eventually, he found himself sitting on the donkey's back, bread and wine in the side bags, and the donkey was moving slowly down the hill, toward town.

There was quite a lot of traffic: donkeys, mule-driven carts, a few horsemen... Not anywhere near as much traffic as... How long ago was it? Could it be just a week or so ago? When he was first entering the city with his whole entourage. Such a festive day, people coming from all over the country for the big holiday celebrations. At that time, it felt like everything was possible.

This was then. Now, Ayshu was trudging along by himself, crippled, alone. His only friends were the donkey which carried him, and the bottle which helped him forget the searing pain from his wounds.

What was there to look forward to in the city? He certainly had no delusions about arousing interest in the city's crowds any more. Faith is fickle. Not only had the city's people lost interest in his predications, they had not even bothered to come see him be crucified.

Besides, what would he talk to them about now? All alone, he now fully deserved the nickname the soldiers had given him as they were nailing him to the cross:
"King of the Few".

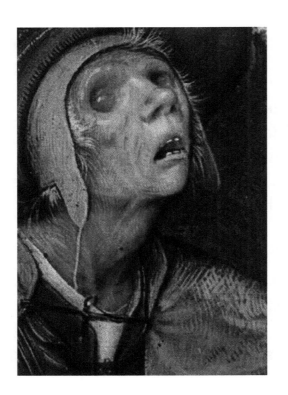

Ayshu felt very angry. But his anger was now overshadowed by sadness—or was it alcohol-induced self-pity? And a lot of fear.

Anger is what got Ayshu to jump from the cross. By now, fear was what got him moving. Fear of staying alone on the deserted hilltop with rapidly dwindling food and drink. Fear of the searing pain that got him to take a swig of wine every so often.

Underneath this fear, there was despair. What's there to look forward to? He had lost any delusions he ever had about the benevolence of his Father, how he'd finally manifest Himself and make it all come to be all right.

What did he now have to look forward to? A man with no home, no money, no friends and no job. A man crippled by overwhelming pain that only abates when his belly is full of wine—and he had hardly any wine left.

No shelter, no food, no money, and no marketable skill.

All these years, he'd been able to do without a job because there were always people to feed and house him. Because they wanted to hear his message of hope. They'd feed him, and somehow they'd feel they had gotten the better of the deal, because he'd given them a taste of eternal life and hope.

Now that he'd lost all hope, what did he have to give that others would give him food for?

Ayshu came to understand that the only occupation his previous life had prepared him for was to be a beggar.

Ayshu found one of the big marketplaces, slid off the donkey's bag, and sat down in such a way as to prominently display his wounds.

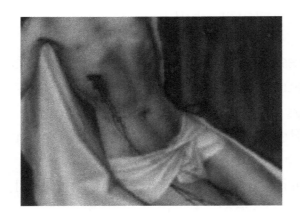 He didn't have to wait long before the first coin fell into his lap. The guy who had thrown it came closer to him, as if inspecting chattel he had just bought.

He seemed fascinated by the large wounds on Ayshu's hands and feet, and poked into one of them. Ayshu howled, at which the guy startled, then poked into another one.

Ayshu howled again.

By now, there was a small crowd around Ayshu. The guy who had poked the wounds turned to the audience as if to say "This is the real thing". And the circle around them kept growing.

Some of the onlookers were passionately discussing how such wounds could come about. There were many opinions, but on one thing there was a consensus: if these were self-inflicted, they reflected a much higher level of dedication than was customary for beggars in these parts. This created a certain measure of respect for Ayshu. A few more people even threw some coins at him. This is how, crippled, Ayshu attracted so much more attention from the city's crowds than he had as a dashing, charismatic preacher.

It was dusk when he got back to the hilltop where he had been crucified. The three crosses still stood against the sky. The middle one was devoid of a body, of course. But so were the others: buzzards had picked at the flesh, and the bones had fallen on the ground.

Ayshu crawled under the tent and took one last swig of wine. Free, at last, from the harassment of the Father, he fell asleep.

He didn't want to leave the tent—the only safe place he knew. But he had to go back to town, buy more wine and some bread with the coins he had, and get more coins. He had to have more wine, or he'd die.

So, once again, he rode into town. And once again, he found a busy marketplace and sat down, marketing his wounds.

When people were throwing coins at him, it was as if they were saying "Better you than me". As if there was a finite sum of human suffering, and seeing him so afflicted accounted for a sizable chunk of it, making it less likely that they, the onlookers, would be afflicted.

He was letting them feel smug and superior to the human wreck he was, and this is how he earned his keep.

It was not altogether bad. He was making enough to buy wine, and bread, and more wine... And the wine was good at dulling the pain, physical and other. It kept the Father's voice at bay.

But the pain made it hard to ride the donkey all the way back to the hilltop. Maybe he could meet other destitute people and find a spot to sleep in the city.

So, instead of leaving the marketplace as soon as the merchants started to leave, he waited. He looked around for other beggars. As expected, there were quite a few. They had now stopped begging, and were scurrying around the marketplace, looking for leftover scraps of food.

When it was very clear that every last edible bit had been found, and eaten, the paupers started leaving, one after another, forming a long line of pathetic figures. Ayshu climbed on his donkey and followed.

He was the only one in the procession to have a donkey. As destitute as he felt, he was looked upon as an object of envy. His hope of establishing bonds of friendship based on a common misfortune evaporated. Instead, he had to worry about protecting his property. There was a time when Ayshu would have gladly given away his coat or his donkey, seeing it as an obstacle to making human contact. But how could he do so now? Without the donkey to carry him, he would die.

The caravan finally stopped in a field, the place in town where the homeless would congregate. Not that they were allowed to. But, hounded as they were from every other part of town, this ended up being sort of a refuge of last resort, and the sheer number of them intimidated the authorities from entering the park.

Ayshu tied a rope from one of the donkey's hind legs to one of his own legs before he lied down to sleep, his head on top of the bag that carried his precious bread and wine.
During the night, he felt a tug on his leg. Somebody was trying to pull the donkey. Ayshu shouted "Stop that!".

The shadow laughed: "And what are you going to do about it, cripple?"

"I'm not gonna let you."

The shadow laughed even more, and moved closer to Ayshu to start to untie the knot on his leg—why waste a perfectly good string by cutting it? Why not take it with the donkey?

Ayshu screamed, took the bottle from his bag, holding it by the

bottleneck, and broke it against a rock in the ground. Now waving his sharp weapon, he hit the man's neck savagely, repeatedly, then the heart, the belly, then the face, lacerating the flesh, until, suddenly exhausted, he lied down and closed his eyes, the bottle still in his right hand.

Rumor of the carnage rapidly spread through the field. By dawn, rare was the park dweller who hadn't heard about it. And, by then, the battle had taken epic proportions. Ayshu's savagery had been directed at more than just one opponent, it was a small army that had attacked this cripple—and look what he'd done to them: there was surely enough blood and body parts around the sleeping Ayshu to support that story.

When he woke up, Ayshu found himself surrounded by a fearful, respectful group ready to make allegiance to him.

Someone handed him a bottle of wine—unbroken, full of wine—as a peace offering. He took a few gulps, then passed it around. When people saw that this fearless leader could also be generous, shouts of relief and joy erupted among the crowd.

Ayshu was now consecrated King of the Underworld.

All his life, Ayshu had looked up to Heaven, listening to the Word from Above instead of the Gut.

It took unbearable pain for him to finally notice that he had a body, that he actually *was* a body, as opposed to spirit made flesh. A body deformed by pain and addicted to wine.

What his fellow beggars acclaimed was not the Spirit made flesh.

It was another kind of spirit—pluck— that came from the trials of the flesh.

About the author:

Thomas A. Kempis is a long-time student of embodied mythology and the collective implicit.

Published by Pausefully books:

http://pausefully.com

9 781892 482310